THE
WITCH'S HEART

THE
WITCH'S HEART

ASHLEY REED

Minute Fiction

ISBN-13: 978-1-7323323-5-5

Cover art: Hilary Bidlake
Special thanks to Lily Prasuethsut, Mara Kanbergs, Blake Howe, Sophia Lawhead, Christina Sanchez, and Jason Torfin

Printed in the United States of America
First Edition

Acknowledgements

For Hilary Bidlake—my editor, artist, and friend—who's been part of this story since it was a few hastily scribbled notes. Thank you for listening while I went on at length about every intricate detail, and for giving as good as you got!

"But anything was better than this agony! Anything was more tolerable than this derision! I could bear those hypocritical smiles no longer! I felt that I must scream or die! and now —again! —hark! louder! louder! louder! louder! 'Villains!' I shrieked, 'dissemble no more! I admit the deed! —tear up the planks! here, here! —It is the beating of his hideous heart!'"

- Edgar Allan Poe,
The Telltale Heart

"And now here is my secret, a very simple secret: it is only with the heart that one can see rightly; what is essential is invisible to the eye."

- Antoine de Saint-Exupéry,
The Little Prince

Hearne didn't know where the glowing ball of glass was leading him. Panting, he stumbled through the undergrowth, the sphere in his hands making menacing shadows of unfamiliar trees. The soft golden light at its center pulsed as he rushed deeper into the blackened woods. He still hadn't the faintest idea what it meant, but he was powerless against the sound the sphere made, the screams that grew louder as its light grew brighter. The voice—that voice—crying out for him.

A hunter with his wits about him would have noticed that the crack of twigs beneath his own boots was the only sound to break the unnatural silence of these woods. He also would have noticed the figure hidden in the shadows ten paces ahead. But Hearne was lost in those sobbing echoes.

He almost lost his footing as the sphere's light

caught on a ghostly man, hair and face white as the remains of a smoldered campfire. Hearne leapt back, slipping in the mud, raising the sphere like a glittering cudgel.

The man was unmoved, still as a gargoyle and twice as menacing. "She waits," he said, his voice smooth, as though he spoke from a throat made of velvet. With one delicate hand, he gestured further into the trees, a veil of darkened leaves and branches obscuring what lay beyond. Hearne sniffed and blinked the sweat from his eyes.

A hunter with his wits about him would have known better than to obey. With quiet sobs filling his mind, Hearne straightened and strode into the dark.

There was nothing here but the dark and the cold. No singing birds, no scritch of squirrels in the trees, no rustling leaves or trickling creeks. Nothing that would have made Asha feel at ease, like she would back home. The sound of ferns swishing around her ankles and her feet meeting packed earth were all Asha heard as she ducked between black, gnarled trees. They jutted toward the sky, creating a canopy so thick that everything beneath was swathed in perpetual night. Between them, silence drifted like fog. She drew her coat up tight around her, but couldn't escape the feeling of spindly, frozen fingers tracing the back of her neck.

She only realized how fast she was moving—trying to escape those creeping claws—when a root caught her toe. Screeching, she pitched through a wall of brambles and was instantly overwhelmed by light. When she had blinked the shine out of her eyes, she found herself at the forest's edge, its dark growth fading into a dull grey field. It stretched for a mile or more before ending at a rocky cliff with a great tower perched on its edge.

Wincing at the sting her fall left behind, Asha squinted at the strange sight. She hadn't seen many towers in her life, but this one was still clearly unusual: curling into a spiral like a braided rope of silvery stone, it stretched so high it disappeared into the cloudy grey sky. She was miles from home, but as tall as it was, she was sure she could have seen a tower this size from the village. So why hadn't she?

But she put that out of her mind quickly. She had come here looking for a witch, and that seemed a likely place to find one.

The walk to the tower felt like it took a dog's age—with only hazy light to go by, time felt muddy and unsteady. Yet when she reached the tower, finding an ornate door of pale wood as tall as three men awaiting her, she still hadn't come up with something to say. How did you talk to a witch? Did they speak human tongue? Or was it like the storybooks said, and they could only snarl and coo at children they wanted to eat?

Asha was no child—she was a full year past ten now—but her stomach still rolled as she stood in front of the great door, eyes grazing over black iron flourishes pounded into the shape of thorns. She was choking down her fear like a thick piece of gristle when the door suddenly disappeared. Or, no—everything disappeared, and she was somewhere else.

Her gasp echoed off vaulted ceilings in a massive hall of white stone. Thick pillars, twisted like the tower itself, stretched high overhead, and a marble floor pierced with lightning bolts of black shone beneath her feet. Rows of stern-looking statues lined the walls, ice-white heads rising out of coal-black armor.

Asha looked this way and that, mesmerized. Only after several long moments did she realize she wasn't alone.

Before her, the hall's polished tiles bled into a sturdy darkwood table curved in the shape of a horseshoe. It held strong under a strange collection of trinkets: slumping piles of rolled parchment, faded golden scales, vials of strangely pale liquid and dozens of worn books in between. A willowy woman wrapped in a red tunic bowed over the table's far end, white hair pouring down her back and two black ram horns sprouting from her head. She lifted a piece of leather covered with strange etchings, studied it, then turned and walked to another stretch of table. She didn't so much as glance at Asha.

Asha was starting to think the woman—witch, definitely a witch—hadn't noticed her. Then she cleared her elegant throat.

"What is it?" said the witch. Her voice was soft, yet so cold it pierced through Asha like an icicle. Asha stammered, wringing her hands in her breeches, words flitting away from her like birds after a misfired arrow. She felt suddenly small and unimpressive—hunting leathers covered in muck, dusty-brown hair falling in her face, eyes wide over cold-paled cheeks—and it robbed her of her words.

"I'm lookin' for my brother," she managed.

"And what business is that of mine?" the witch said coolly, not looking away from the colorful powder she was measuring.

"He went into the black woods," Asha stammered. "They say there's a witch there—I mean here. Who controls things. I thought you might..."

The witch let out a low hum, sounding almost amused. A shiver ran up Asha's back. "Many souls traipse through my forest. Their fate is no concern of mine. Now leave. You are disturbing my work."

"He—he knows never to come here," Asha pleaded. "They're forbidden—the woods—and he's a hunter, he—he knows his own forest better—"

The witch sighed like she had accidentally spilled some powder or could not decipher a hard-to-read scribble. Lifting a delicate arm, she gracefully traced a finger through the air.

A deafening clack echoed off the ceiling, and Asha whirled to find the statues that lined the hall weren't statues at all—they were people, moving unnaturally slow, staves cracking against the floor as they stepped toward her in unison. Her stomach clenched.

"Please!" she screeched, backing away as the men advanced. "Please—I just want to find Hearne and, and I'm sure you know the forest and—"

The witch had already lifted her hand, and the legion of statues froze at her slightest twitch. She turned her gaze to Asha, and Asha found unnatural, vibrant gold eyes that fixed her to the spot.

"Hearne is your brother," she said. Asha could tell it wasn't a question. "Yes. I called him here."

"How?" Asha gulped, shock overcoming her fear. "Why?"

"That is not your concern," the witch said. "And I will not have you interrupt his work, either."

Asha winced. Slowly, she glanced around the hall. She couldn't imagine the witch needing her brother's help—not when she had a statue army at her command. "I won't," she answered. "I just want to see him. Do—d'you know where he is?"

The witch's eyes narrowed. Asha felt that cold, prying feeling again, like she was a carcass being picked over on the work table.

"Very well," the witch said. She waved indistinctly as she bent over her scroll once more. "You. Attend to her."

Asha couldn't tell who the witch was talking to, but the statue men had no such trouble. One just as straight-backed and stone-faced as the rest stepped forward, modestly bowing his head to the witch before drifting toward Asha.

Asha tensed and reached for the knife at her hip. The statue-man didn't even twitch, stopping wordlessly an arm's length away. Up close she saw he had the same brilliant white hair as the witch, and his black robes were trimmed with glimmering silver. It looked like the witch had an army of dolls.

"Young miss," the doll-man said, gesturing behind her, his sudden wisp of a voice making Asha jump.

When she turned, she found the great grey field outside the tower stretching before her, its chill sweeping through her hair and coat. When she swung back around, the tower door stood before her again. The statue-man, standing straight and tall at her side, stared at her blandly.

They were nearly back across the plain, the forest yawning to fill her view, when the silence became too much. "What's your name?" she asked. "I'm Asha. Of Clan Baar."

The doll-man stared ahead. She swore his head didn't even bob with his steps; he could have balanced a stack of the witch's books on his head. "Pallas," he said slowly, sounding unfamiliar with the word.

"Okay," Asha said suspiciously. She wondered if he made it up. "So... you're going to help me find my brother?"

Elegantly, he reached into the folds of his robes and extracted a glass bauble almost too large to hold with one hand. It was round and clear, covered with ridges and swirls that looked like bird feathers. She could see a dim curl of light reflected in its center, though with such a grey sky above she couldn't tell where it was drawing light from.

"With this," he confirmed, holding the ball

out to her. "I will attend to you. It is dangerous to brave the forest alone."

"What's it do?" Asha asked, taking the ball and cradling it delicately in her palms. It didn't feel particularly magical.

Pallas nodded toward the trees, just a few meters ahead of them now, and said nothing else. She glared, lip twitching—back home he'd be left to cart the supplies and defend himself from wolves if he couldn't bother to communicate. But as she stepped into the chilly shade of tangled branches, she realized he was her entire hunting party on uncharted ground. She swallowed thickly.

The bauble came to life as she stepped into the shadows. At first she thought it was the change in the light, but then she felt it pulse against her palms, a whisper of sound escaping its glossy shell. She took another few steps. It got a bit brighter, its beat a half-second faster.

She was entirely in the forest's shade, twigs crunching underfoot, when she noticed Pallas wasn't following her. He stood at the edge of the tree line, peering wordlessly at the branches above.

"What? You comin'?"

"Every time I enter this forest," he said dreamily, "I wonder if I will ever return. I suppose you should wonder the same."

Asha stared. Slowly, Pallas lowered his gaze and gave her a small smile.

The ball's light did a bit of good puncturing the dark, clearing a path so every dug-up root didn't look like crooked claws reaching for her ankle. Otherwise, it was useless. Its pulse was weak and hard to detect, its glow growing intense one moment then dying to a glimmer the next.

"How does this track anythin'?" she groused, shaking it like a broken clock.

"You are a hunter, are you not? Like your brother?" Pallas said. He drifted along, untouched by a single branch or smear of mud. "I'm sure your skills will serve you well here."

"This is different," Asha snapped back, feeling her cheeks heat. "You can guess what an animal's goin' to do easier'n a human." She wasn't about to admit that she was still learning how to track, that Hearne—a full seventeen years older and more seasoned—was supposed to be training her. She'd only figured out he'd disappeared into the witch's woods when he didn't meet her that morning, bow in hand, for their daily hunt.

Shoving her way through a high wall of bushes, Asha stumbled into an unseen puddle and cursed as it soaked through her boots. "Why would the witch even need help?" she grumbled, yanking them off to dump the water out. "This is her forest. She can just use magic to find whatever she wants, can't she?"

"Her Magnificence is not all-powerful," Pallas answered as he appeared, pristine, beside her. "The forest has a magic of its own. Not all here is beholden to her."

Asha squinted at him. She didn't know any-thing about magic, especially dark magic, but she wouldn't be surprised if this dark and silent place was full of it. It was nothing like Clan Baar's forest, a welcoming swath of dense greenery to the west of the village, miles away from the black wood to the east. Their forest was always full of the prints and gouges of animal life, plus the vivid plants and musical insects that fed it. This place was empty, cold, and felt like it was keeping secrets. Knowing there were things about it even the witch didn't know made Asha shiver.

"Why not send one of you then?" she asked.

Pallas paused, and she saw his eyes narrow like he was trying to balance the right words on his tongue. "The quarry your brother pursues is formidable. Besting it requires a certain tempera-ment and skills that we do not possess," he finally said. "Her Magnificence requested he attend to it personally."

It was Asha's turn to stare as her mouth twist-ed into a grimace. "Why?" she finally snapped. "How would she know him? How would you know any of us?"

Pallas' face stayed blank, and he made no move to answer. She was an inch from pulling the knife from her belt and making him speak when her ears caught a soft, faraway sound, like rain on the forest leaves. That was already odd in this quiet place, but then it grew vast, moving like a wall of sound from the west. As she listened, it grew from a whisper to a ground-shaking racket—then a vast stretch of the shadowy forest floor surged forward, skittering directly toward her.

With a yelp, Asha latched onto the nearest tree, digging her fingers into the damp bark and pulling herself onto a low branch. As she climbed higher, the shivering wave of dark passed below her, oblivious to her presence. This close she could see that it wasn't a wave at all, but a crush of inky creatures no bigger than field hares. Their limbs were bent at sharp, broken angles, their small bodies covered with golden bubbles that pulsed with a sharp inner light. No two creatures had the same number.

She gaped, clinging harder to a thick branch, her head swinging as she scanned the bushes for any sign of Pallas. She didn't spot a single wisp of white hair. She was just about to shout for him when a resounding crunch echoed through the trees. Another followed, then another, as loud as cannon blasts or tree trunks snapping. Asha barely dared to turn her head.

At first she saw only darkness, until a piece of it quivered and a gangly arm emerged into the light. Knotted claws spasmed as the arm crashed down, carrying a body as great as a grizzly bear, but thin and twisted at painful angles like its bones had been broken a dozen times. It was covered in gold bubbles, some bigger than Asha's head, and they wriggled with each crashing step. Most were near where its head should have been. Eyes, Asha realized numbly as the creature twitched and clicked toward her.

Every animal shriek in Asha's brain cried for

her to run, but there was no time to move before it lumbered under her branch. Fighting to quiet her shaking breath, she stayed as still as she could, willing herself to be invisible.

The creature froze as it passed, tilting its head back like a hound listening for its mark. Only then did Asha hear a soft humming growing around her, stretching into the still leaves above. It sounded like a voice. For a moment, she thought it was the beast itself—then terror, sharp and cold, stabbed through her gut. The voice was coming from the bag on her back.

She didn't stop to consider the impossibility of it. Arm shaking and tongue impaled between her teeth, she slowly pulled one of the straps off her shoulder. Below, the creature let out a shrill snarl— even that was twisted, like a roar and a shriek coiled together.

The bag's leather strap caught on her elbow. Asha choked a sob against her fist as the voice grew louder and louder.

With a last, desperate tug, she ripped the whispering thing free and dropped it from the branch. The sack landed in the undergrowth with a hollow thunk and the creature spun to face it, impossibly fast for its size. The voice was so loud now that it easily pierced through the green. Only an unnatural, echoing gurgle from the monster overpowered it.

Long talons plucked the leather open—didn't grab and shake it or tear it open like any other animal would—and clumsily dragged the ball out.

The sphere glowed a brilliant yellow-white. Echoing laughter tumbled from it, words Asha could actually hear as the creature's claws closed around it. *See it? Aingael, look!*

The beast's head shot up like it had been kicked under the chin. Its eyes were empty globules of gold, but Asha could still feel them burning into her like a blacksmith's chisel. Slowly, it rose onto its warped hind legs, wrapping its foreclaws around the branch on either side of her.

With a scream Asha threw herself back, tumbling out of the tree and landing hard on the ground below. A shot of pain tore through her leg, but fear overwhelmed it. She scrambled to her feet and drew her knife. Screeching like no animal she'd ever heard—nearly bird, nearly elk—the creature sank to the ground and reached for her with its wicked claws.

An arrow lodged in the thin branch of its arm. Squealing, it snapped the limb back, trying to pry the shaft free. Another buried itself in the coil of its shoulder.

A black mass raced from the shadows in the arrow's wake. As it strode into the light, the mass became Hearne, bow drawn, steady-handed as he nocked another arrow.

The world moved quickly. Hearne let the arrow fly, piercing one of the creature's slimy eyes. It wailed and skittered back as viscous golden fluid dribbled from the wound. Asha scrambled back as Hearne hooked the bow over his shoulder and drew his sword, slashing at the creature's head.

The beast reeled onto its hind legs and Asha felt the quaking in her bones as it slammed down to the earth. Hearne dodged expertly and slashed again. Asha expected the creature to push back, unleash the brutal animal strength its wiry body promised. But instead, it fell back. Leaping out of Hearne's reach, it shuffled, cowed, before springing away into the dark. The crunch of heavy footfalls echoed in its wake.

Hearne tensed to chase it, then stopped, swearing under his breath. As he straightened and sheathed his sword, he turned and scanned the shadows that encased her. "Asha?"

Relief flooded her like warm tea in this frozen wood. He looked a mess—leathers covered in mud, dark splotches under his eyes, mop of brown hair filthy and short beard unkempt—but he stood tall with all his limbs accounted for.

Her stomach untwisted all at once as she scrambled to her feet and crashed into him. She waited for him to lift her from the ground like a twig or a feather for a proper embrace—but it didn't come. The hands that found her shoulder and the top of her head were kind, but the sigh that found her ears was not. "Hell's teeth, don't tell me ya followed me," he said.

"W—" Asha stammered, angry heat rising up to her ears. She jerked back and punched him in the shoulder. "Why else would I be here, hound-shaft?"

Hearne breathed deeply and carefully. He was tall and thin by Baar standards (that is what made him a superior archer, their cousins would grumble), but still had hints of the clan's sturdy birthright: wide shoulders, thick arms, height that Asha refused to envy. He was always calm, like a great bear that had nothing to fear from the world around it. So when he sighed like that, she knew he was feeling something fierce—and she was about to get a lecture on it.

He took her by the shoulders. "Are ya hurt?"

"No," she lied. Her knee stung, but she ignored it.

"Good," he said before kneeling down to look her in the eye. "But ya shouldn't have come. And ya can't stay."

With a grunt she flung his hands away. "I'm not goin' home without you!" she snapped. "Why'd you run away? Why're you helpin' the witch?"

She could see thoughts churning behind his eyes before they narrowed. "Ya spoke to her? Are ya tryin' to get turned into a frog?"

"Only after you did! And she said you were helpin' her. Why?"

He dragged a hand over his stubbled face. "I'd burn a whole fire down explainin'," he groaned distantly. His eyes were unfocused, like he wasn't truly talking to her.

"Then I'll come with you," Asha said. "Let me help!"

"No," he chastised. She felt like a mutt that had gnawed on its master's catch. He ducked his chin, hand to his face, surely lost in thoughts of how to get her home. Then they caught on something over her shoulder.

Asha didn't notice the flowing white shape drifting close until it was beside her. She whirled. Freshly emerged from the brush and impossibly clean, Pallas gazed at Hearne, expressionless.

"She sent a damned escort?" Hearne chuckled, shaking his head. "Dunno what ya mistress is playin' at, but might as well make use of ya. Take my sister home. And tell your witch it's part of our bargain."

Asha's insides tightened. "No!" she shouted. "If you think he can take me anywhere, you got orts for brains."

Right then, Asha thought she would rather be the wobbly-eyed creature. Hearne's sighs and the impatient furrow of his brows were worse than his arrows. "Go home, Asha. I'll explain everything soon. I swear."

Her eyes fell, glaring divots into the dirt. He reached for her shoulder and she slapped his hand away. For a second, they were both quiet.

"Ya both know the way," he said, even and untouched. "Tread sure."

He had said that to her a thousand times before—guiding her into the delicate racket of their forest, sending her after her first stag, trying to keep the grin from his face as he pulled her out of a lake. But it seemed like a different person saying it now. One who turned with a deer's swiftness, agile steps carrying him away.

Asha's head shot up as he disappeared into the dark. "Wait!" she cried. But as she tried to run after, her knee screeched with pain and rooted her feet.

Soon there wasn't even a shadow left of him as she stared, throat dry and aching, into the dark.

Her throat ached even more when she let out a wrathful scream that bounced off every leaf before dying to nothing, useful as a snuffed spark.

She heard the delicate crunch of grass behind her and whipped around. Pallas was still there, looking at her with that same vacant look. Or, no—his mouth took no shape and his nose didn't twitch out of place, but his eyes were too wide, his eyebrows too high.

Asha glowered at him, then snatched her rucksack from the brush and limped after Hearne's tracks.

"It did not attack you," Pallas said matter-of-factly. With a satisfying crack, Asha snapped a handful of twigs and dropped them onto their blossoming campfire, nearly smothering it with their weight.

"You might've missed it," she said snottily as she coaxed the flame back to life with a few light puffs and strips of bark. "You were hidin' like a coward."

"If it had meant to harm you, your corpse would have fallen out of that tree," Pallas challenged.

The dark was even more oppressive after sunset, an impenetrable onyx wall that enclosed their circle of firelight. She almost took comfort in it, like nothing could break through to reach them. The fire grew with a soft ballad of crackles, lighting Pallas' face sharply. She couldn't read it any better.

"Then what was it doin'?" she said smugly, curling her fingers like the beast curled its claws. She gave him an eerie, gnarled wave. "Comin' to say hello?"

"I do not know. But it is dangerous. That is the creature Her Magnificence wishes culled."

Asha said nothing, pulling a strip of hardtack out of her bag and gnawing on it fiercely. Her wrist bumped against the glass ball, dark now with barely a glimmer at its center. Even looking at it set her teeth on edge.

"Your brother was not happy to see you," Pallas observed. Asha stiffened, then pointedly ignored him. "If I am to abide by his wishes, I would return you home."

"Wanna try?" Asha growled. She may not have been as strong as Hearne, but Pallas was about as sturdy as a paper doll.

"No. I take orders from none but Her Magnificence," he answered evenly. "But why do you insist on pursuing him, knowing he finds your presence distasteful?"

"Why d'you insist on talking so much?" Asha snapped, bristling. "I find that *distasteful.*"

"I simply wish to understand. This is... irregular."

"Oh, you think so?" she barked back. "You know

what? I wish to understand, too." Jamming a hand into her bag, she tossed the ball at him. He caught it with disappointing ease. "How 'bout you do some explainin'. Why'd that thing start talkin'? And what does it have to do with the monster and what does that have to do with my brother?"

Pallas turned the ball over, shifting it back and forth like he meant to weigh it in his palms. He was stalling.

"Well?" she demanded.

"This object," he said, his gaze locked on its textured surface, "is sensitive to memories. It is drawn to them, and the beings by which they are held. It can be tuned to one soul by proper magic— Her Magnificence is the only one with such skill. But even then, it can be overwhelmed." He held it out to her. "I believe stronger memories interfered."

"Then whose memories were those?" she asked as she took it back, turning the ball over herself. It felt unremarkable now, dark and silent and tangible as it reflected the orange firelight. "I heard a human voice."

"I do not know. This forest holds many such mysteries."

"Thanks," Asha snipped, though she was too distracted to put in the proper bite. "Fine. Then why was the monster so caught up with it?"

"You were quite enamored with it at first sight, as I recall."

"I'm not a beast," she said sharply, in case it didn't occur to this puffed-up blueblood. "Beasts don't understand human talk. Or they aren't supposed to. That one did. I think. What were those things, anyway? They weren't normal animals."

"Hmm. They are... strange creatures." He smoothed his sleeves delicately, drifting away in thought. "That much you have noticed, but I can offer little else. They are beastly yet inquisitive, guided by animal urges but not mindless. They are aware and unaware by turn, particularly the great one." He looked at her suddenly, his gaze piercing. "You are lucky the turns fell in your favor."

So they were like wolves or bears. Asha wasn't as impressed as he wanted her to be. "And my brother? What's any of this got to do with him?"

"Her Magnificence believes he can slay the great beast where all others have failed," Pallas answered, his tone a shrug. "He seems a skilled hunter. Is that your understanding as well?"

Asha bristled. He knew she wouldn't argue. "Could she have... I don't know, magicked him or something?" she tried instead, absently putting a larger branch on the fire. "I get what she wants, but... I don't get why he's goin' along. He's got no reason. And he's not actin' normal."

"It is possible. But bewitched souls are rarely so willful. I believe your brother is here of his own accord."

Asha slumped, flopping onto her sleeping roll and shoving the ball back in her bag. "If that thing's so dangerous that even the witch is scared of it," she mumbled, "how could my brother kill it?" She felt her gut twist with something new and ugly, something that felt worse than anger.

Pallas paused so long that Asha thought he had fallen asleep. She was beginning to drift off herself when he spoke. "I believe there is something unique about your brother," he said. "But only he and Her Magnificence truly know what it is."

He sounded, Asha thought, like he was caught in a net, stifled as he pressed against it and found no give. When she rolled over to look at him, he had risen to his feet, brushing wrinkles from his robe. "I will keep watch for the night. Good evening."

Asha made to call him back, but in a blink he disappeared into the dark as quickly and completely as a shadow. Sighing, she laid down and drifted off with the vague hope that she wouldn't wake half-eaten.

She was lucky—something besides animal teeth roused her. A soft glow and a softer murmur prodded her awake, and with bleary eyes she found specks of light pricking through her rucksack. Struggling through a cocoon of sleep, she plunged a hand into her bag and dragged the ball of light out.

There was something inside, she realized as she pulled it close. Flowers and grass. A small hand jutted forward as if it was her own, like was looking through another's eyes. In its palm hovered a small pink butterfly—no, not a real one. It was pale and gritty, like it was made of sand. It crumbled and the one holding it—a little girl—giggled joyfully.

Asha hugged the ball closer as a great, flowering field and a summer-blue sky filled it, trying to take in every detail. The girl ducked clumsily, creeping through the grass. A few feet ahead was a boy with light brown hair—bow in hand, back straight, arrow pulled taut.

Snickering, the girl shoved him from behind. His arrow flew wildly off course, and Asha flinched as he cried out and nearly toppled. He spun around, cheeks pink and voice high as he shouted, "What'dya do that for?"

It was Hearne. Asha felt like she'd fallen out of the tree again. He was much smaller, younger than Asha was now, but there was no mistaking the mop of hair or the harsh nose. He shoved the girl back and the image shook wildly as she let out a high-pitched sob.

It started to fade. Asha swore under her breath, shaking the ball roughly. It snapped to something new—two hands joined together, a mortar and pestle, a baby wrapped in swaddling cloth—then the ball went dark.

Her lip twisted. She wondered if she'd broken it. But that was quickly replaced with another thought: what she had just seen was surely a memory, like Pallas had said. One strong enough to get the sphere's attention, or something like that. But... where had it come from?

She lay back down, her wide eyes no match for

the surrounding wall of night. She couldn't see a thing. But she got the sharp, prickling feeling that something out in the quiet could see her.

"What do you intend to do when you find your brother?" Pallas asked, his voice jarring in the dawn air. "I do not imagine he will be happy to see you."

Dew splashed across Asha's face as she shoved aside a wayward branch. It didn't do much to wake her. "He can chew rocks," she grumbled. "I'm goin' with him whether he wants me to or not."

"He seems perfectly capable of caring for himself."

"Ugh, why do you always talk so much?"

Her pack weighed heavy on her shoulders, the ball pulling down on her like a stone. It made no sound and gave off no light. She wished it would, even if it was bound to attract something nasty. That would at least prove that what she had seen last night—what had kept her from getting a wink of sleep—wasn't a dream.

They scaled a slope blanketed in ferns, grey streaks of light jutting through the leaves overhead. The few tracks Hearne had left had disappeared miles back (like he'd meant them to, she thought bitterly). Asha wiped her eyes and tried to concentrate, feeling for any vibration against her back that meant the ball sensed something.

"Have you given any thought to why Her Magnificence might have called upon him?" Pallas' voice cracked the quiet like a boot on the surface of a frozen pond.

Hitching the bag up on her shoulders, Asha walked faster. "Why? You didn't care yesterday."

Infuriatingly, Pallas kept up. "As you may recall, the great beast behaved strangely toward you. I expect it responded to some characteristic which you and your brother share. A certain bearing or balance of humors. Perhaps an enchantment placed upon your line. Uncommon, but not implausible. Can you think what it might be?"

"How 'bout you go and ask your witch," Asha snapped, then broke into a sprint. "I'm goin' ahead!"

She tore into a cluster of dark ivy and thick trunks further up the slope. Vaulting over rocks and running along downed trees, she tried to leave the slightest tracks possible so Pallas couldn't follow her. She didn't need a nursemaid, especially a nosy one.

But even if he didn't follow, his words did, latching like a wicked-beaked bird onto her ear. No one could question her clan's hunting skill—not while Baar furs and boots kept them warm—and for all her uncles' and cousins' guffing there was no doubt Hearne was the best. Maybe it was magic, though that made her nose wrinkle. Hearne had been training her to hunt for years, always hovering a few feet back as she read tracks, wore her arms out nocking arrows, and chased injured quarries through tangled underbrush. She loved the thrill of a successful hunt; she could all but feel his hand on her shoulder, congratulating her on a well-won prize. But it was still hard, painful, grimy work, and she didn't like the thought of waving that away with magic.

And besides, they hunted stags and lynxes and in a lucky season a gods-gifted bear, not monsters. Hearne never felled anything they couldn't use or trade—and he definitely didn't do any of it because a witch told him to.

Asha didn't notice how smooth the rock was beneath her feet until they came out from under her. Squawking, she tumbled to the ground, then scrambled up and kicked the rock free. Her shoulders heaved with angry breaths as she watched it disappear into the undergrowth.

A furious shriek was growing in her throat. Damn Hearne, damn the witch, damn everyone! But just as it was about to rip free, her eyes rose, and surprise silenced it.

Tucked into the trees before her was—something. A glowing blue tree, trunk covered with what looked like half-melted ice, emerged from a glittering pool. On its branches perched glowing yellow bubbles, blobby and viscous like frogspawn. Inside them she could see snatches of flashing shapes, and as she moved forward she heard bits of whispered noise. Sometimes the shapes looked like humans and animals. Sometimes they looked like nothing at all.

Glancing down at the strange pool, she toed the surface with her boot. She cringed when it stuck to the leather, dripping thickly like porridge. More shapes, most of them impossible to identify, drifted beneath the surface.

"Ah, you discovered one," came Pallas' voice by her ear.

Asha nearly tripped into the pool. She swung and glared when she found him standing serenely at her shoulder. How had she not heard him coming? But she pushed the thought away in favor of the pool and tree. "One what?"

"A growth," he said casually, as if it was no more interesting than a puddle or patch of weeds. "Your sphere was retrieved from one such as this."

Suddenly, Asha realized she could feel a faint vibration against her back. She ripped the bag off her shoulders and found the ball blazing like a small sun. Maybe it was reacting to the tree? Still, it looked too neat and symmetrical to have grown here, or anywhere.

"But what is it?" she asked. As she watched the flickers of images overhead, strange feelings burrowed into her stomach—bubblings of curiosity, prickly fear, chilly loneliness. All soft and muted, like she was remembering things she'd felt ages ago but had mostly forgotten.

"A manifestation of sorts. We believe they form where the creatures you saw gather often."

"Like a nest?"

"That could be, though they are not known to breed."

The flickering shades inside one bubble coiled into some kind of shape. Now Asha was watching two hands, warped slightly by the orb's curved face, grinding berries and leaves with a mortar and pestle. It was like seeing through someone else's eyes again. The hands—thin, feminine and calloused—paused as their owner turned to a piece of parchment covered in strange etchings.

Asha squinted, then jumped as a mighty crash burst in her ears. It took her a moment to realize that it came from the ball in her hands, but the woman in the bubble seemed to hear it as well. She whipped around, shouts ringing as she stared into the light of a wide-open door.

Asha had to look away when a fresh wound filled the orb, a noxious, two-pronged snake bite that was turning from angry red to sickly purple.

The image changed as the woman looked at the face of the wounded. Asha nearly dropped the sphere. It was Hearne again. He was older this time, with patches of beard on his chin, but nowhere near as old as the Hearne she knew. Breathing hard, he stared at the ceiling, eyes cloudy and unfocused. Asha's own breathing sped, her stomach twisting.

The woman looked at him for a long, unbroken moment. Then her gaze dropped to the wound, dark red seeping through her fingers as they delicately enveloped it. They shook, a soft yellow glow curling around their edges. Asha heard the woman gulping and straining as she squinted against the light.

Then the woman pulled her hands back, drawing streaks of dark purple and red from the wound like grisly threads. When the last grasping vein slid from his skin, she jerked away, letting the noxious liquid splash onto the floor.

The woman looked up to find Hearne's eyes clearing and blinking, his head shifting with the first hints of alertness. Asha felt a lightness spreading through her arms and chest when his eyes finally found the woman's, wide with disbelief.

But then the world inside the orb suddenly pulsed and spun dizzyingly. Asha closed her eyes, and when she opened them again, the woman was lying on the floor, ankles shuffling around her frantically.

"Curious," Pallas said, jerking Asha from the illusion. "Do you recognize this person? She seemed to know your brother."

"No foolin'," Asha muttered. The woman's vision was still blurry, but a head-shaped blob started to take shape in front of her as she was guided upright. "No. And why are we seein' her memories?"

Pallas stared at her, eyebrow raised. It was the most pointed look she'd ever seen on his face. "Truly? Think."

Asha stammered. "I can't even tell what she looks like! How am I supposed to recognize her?" She glanced back at the orb above, squinting and studying, as the blob became an older, dark-haired woman. Asha waved irritably. "She's wearing the Taube crest. They're the village healers. Happy?"

It was true: the familiar Clan Taube dove was embroidered on the older woman's choker, white thread filling out its wings with green bushels of herbs surrounding them. It made more sense the longer Asha thought about it—if anyone could heal a wound like that with nothing but dust and mutters, it would be a Taube. Now that she looked closer, the dark-haired woman looked like Old Woman Gilsi, though a few decades younger. But then Asha kept thinking, and her eyes started to narrow.

"But there aren't any other Taube women," she said slowly. "There's only Old Man Kar and Old Woman Gilsi. And they're both ancient."

Hearne slowly slipped into view, wide-eyed, stammering, more amazed than she'd ever seen him before. The woman chuckled weakly, but happily. Warmth spread up through Asha's arms.

"Who is she?" Asha asked no one.

CRACK. The image vanished with a pop and a jitter, and something else was in its place. Blackness and light spasmed inside the bubble until she could just make out leaves and mud. Trees, thick and dark like the ones around them. A sound grew inside Asha's, a low rumble that shook through the glass and slowly became the sound of a hundred screams—

The beast—whole and real and wailing—burst through the branches of the tree. Screeching, Asha nearly lost her footing as she scrambled back. Globes in the beast's path burst like boils as it flailed and crashed into the viscous water below.

Asha juggled the ball and drew her knife with shaking fingers. That bulbous head wobbled toward her, dripping with thick jelly.

In the same moment Asha realized Pallas was gone—coward!—she remembered what he said. The beast hadn't harmed her before. Maybe if she was calm and careful, it wouldn't—

A shrill squeal tore through the air, and the beast lunged at her in a violent tangle of arms and eyes. She screamed and slashed, catching its gangly limb with her blade. As it jolted back with a pained howl, Asha bolted into the trees.

The darkness pressed against her on every side. The sphere's light was bright, but stark and close, throwing confusing shadows in her path. She battered herself against harsh trunks and rough bark with no idea what lay ahead. But she could hear the beast bounding behind her, filling the forest with its crashing footfalls and wild shrieks.

The ground disappeared beneath Asha's feet. Her shoulder hit hard-packed earth. The sphere flew from her arms. She tumbled helplessly, shrieking when her hip smashed against a rock. For half a moment she fell weightlessly through the air, then crashed to a stop, hitting flat dirt with a slam that ripped every ounce of breath from her chest.

She'd only pulled in a few deep heaves, gasping and choking like she'd never breathed before, when a deeper darkness swallowed her.

The world slipped back in slowly, like wisps of light flitting through a dark cave. Asha thought she was blinking—slowly, sluggishly, like her eyes had been glued shut—but it took time for grey shapes to start emerging from the black. Working an elbow into the dirt, she tried to sit up, then collapsed again at a violent pain in her stomach and knee.

She gulped stale air, lying still as her head swam. She tried to remember where she was. Glancing around, she found a steep hill with a sheer drop at its base, dotted with black lumps of rock and featureless trunks.

A cold jolt shot up her back when she remembered the beast clawing at her heels. She listened close, trying to catch even a hint of its otherworldly screech. But only silence reached her, and a hint of soft blue light through nearby trees.

Asha grimaced. She'd had enough mysterious lights to last her whole life. But the beast had her scent, and there was nothing but dark between them. Even having a dull glow to see by would be something—and, with a quiet swear, she realized the sphere of light was gone. Slowly, she struggled upright, holding her pounding head, and limped toward the gleam.

She braced herself for something unexplainable—ponds with faces or creeks of silver or rocks that talked. Instead she found a crumbling circle of bricks. She was sure it was some sort of wicked shrine until she saw a wooden pail sitting on its lip. An old well.

When she looked around, she found a house poking out of the shadows, blue light drifting through wooden walls caving with rot. Another appeared as her eyes adjusted, then another and another, standing in a ring with the well at its center.

Something moved—a silky shadow floating between the moldering boards. Asha ducked behind the well, then recognized the white hair and the untouched cloak lit by that unearthly glow. She watched Pallas disappear into one of the houses, her squint spreading into a glare.

An aching leg made stalking hard, but she managed to keep her steps quiet as she snuck through a gap in the wall. It didn't matter—a soft cascade of sound, like hundreds of voices whispering at once, poured through the gouge.

Gooseflesh danced across her skin. The same glowing blobs she'd seen before covered the walls, clinging like spider sacks, their gold centers ringed with cold blue. The shadows inside them were even more formless—they piled on each other like mice in a cage, blending and unblending, jolting in tune with the whispers.

Pallas stood a few yards away, a silhouette in the icy light. Asha didn't make a sound or a move toward him. But he looked back anyway, gaze resting on her in a way she felt more than saw. "You escaped," he said mildly.

"Yeah," Asha groused. "Nice of you to come lookin' for me."

"You abandoned me as well," he said, turning away. "There is no need to be bitter."

"Where are we?" she asked, limping after him as he flitted forward. Her eyes caught on overturned chairs around a circular hearth, rusting pots, a pile of linens folded and molding in a woven basket.

A rotten plank cracked under her foot. She jumped back as three of the small monsters from the forest, startled by the sharp sound, skittered past her into new hidey holes.

Pallas wasn't bothered—he moved on, ducking through a collapsed wall and into another house as she hobbled after him. There were more of the creatures here, carpeting the stone floor so it seemed to shiver. He strode into them without a thought, their tiny claws clicking on the wood as they shifted out of his way. Asha winced.

"Pallas," she called, edging along the path he cleared. The creatures scrambled away from her boots, then returned to fill the space she left behind.

More of the globs clung to the ceiling and hissed with hundreds of mutters. One, whispered over and over, pushed through the racket: *Run. Witch. Run! The witch!*

"Pallas!" she finally shouted, reaching out and digging her fingers into one of his silky sleeves. "What is this place?"

He wasn't strong enough to pull away in one jerk, but he managed on a second try. She stood in silence as he wandered away like he hadn't noticed her.

"You know what's goin' on here, don't you?" she said. "You're not tellin' me somethin'!"

He stopped, and it was only then that she saw his hands curling and uncurling, wringing together. "There is much I am not telling you," he said. "Just as there is much you are not telling me."

"Like what?" she snapped. "I told you, I don't know why the witch wants my brother's help. I wanna know, too!"

He shot her a sharp, cold glance. "You presume to tell me you do not know your own kinsman? That the witch would happily receive a strange child and grant her an attendant out of kindness? If you are not a liar, then you are a fool."

"That's not—shut up!" she stammered. "My family—and Hearne, he's not—"

But even as she scrambled for words, new thoughts started leaking in, mucking up her mind. Hearne didn't talk about himself much. No one really did. Everyone else in the village had stories from when they were her age, but even though he was the oldest, no one ever had anything to say about him. Not about the time he nearly died from a snake bite. Not about the girl who saved him.

"He doesn't talk much," she offered weakly. "But I swear, I'm not hiding anything! And if you tell me what you know, maybe we can figure this out."

Pallas stared at her for a long time, like he was trying to drag her thoughts out through her eyes. "Suppose I did. Would you believe me?" he said softly, turning his back to her. "Or would you betray me to the witch?"

Asha's mouth fell open with no words to show for it. She was trying to stammer together a reply when three globes across the room stuttered, a stronger, clearer image filling them.

She stopped. Inside all three stood a woman with high, sharp cheeks, tying her charcoal hair back with a ribbon. She preened strangely, like she was—

Looking in a mirror.

The young Gilsi stood behind her, laughing gleefully. Asha squinted. She looked just like the woman in front of the mirror, except older.

The image changed. Now Asha could see the green of a true forest and hear the slight twitter of birds. A stag ambled into view, and as Asha got closer, she heard a soft gasp of wonder.

The woman turned, and Hearne shifted into view beside her. He was older now, with a fuller beard. Lying on his belly in the dirt and leaves, he drew his bow, eyes sharp and focused.

He let the arrow fly, then swore bitterly—he must have missed. The woman didn't turn to see it. Instead she leaned closer, his face filling her vision. He blinked at her like he'd been hit upside the head with a rock, then shifted closer, eyes closing and head tilting.

A wave of prickling disgust shot down Asha's arms and she looked away. She only risked turning back when she heard dim cheering and found a new picture in the globes: two hands clasped tight, wrapped in cloth embroidered with leaves and arrows.

More globes were filled with the same picture now, so when the woman's gaze rose Asha saw Hearne reflected a dozen times. He wore a dark blue coat with a collar of brown bear fur. He was looking at their encased hands, his smile so wide he almost looked like a different person. The woman lifted her free hand; a small bear made of pink sand appeared in her palm, alongside a pink dove that circled and settled on its head. Hearne chuckled.

"Pallas!" Asha called eagerly, looking away as the woman touched Hearne's cheek and started to lean close. "Hearne had a wife! She was a Taube. But she—"

When Asha turned, Pallas was gone. Trying not to step on any of the skittering creatures underfoot, she shuffled to where she had seen him last. She spotted him not far off, in front of a yawning gap at the end of the hall, stone-still as the first time she met him.

"Pallas?" she said again. He didn't budge. A streak of wetness on his cheek caught the light as she took another step. He sank to his knees, reaching out for something around the corner, shaking like a starving man begging for bread.

One of the small monsters, no different from the others, crept cautiously into view. It tilted its round head at him. Asha watched as Pallas pulled in a shaky breath and smiled.

Outside, a great shadow slid into the gap. Spots of dim gold gleamed in the dark.

Asha gasped. "Pallas!"

The creature's claws crashed into his back, flinging him against the wall. He collapsed in a heap and the wood followed, tumbling down on the beast's brittle arm. With a gargled shriek it disappeared behind a cascade of moss and decay.

Her foot nearly punched through the floor as she raced to Pallas' side. He lifted his head, eyes cloudy with shock. "Come on!" she screamed, grabbing his thin arm. He felt shockingly light as she hauled him to his feet.

He followed her for a few clumsy steps, his wrist limp in her hand. Then a jolt shot through her and she nearly lost her footing—his arm, suddenly hard as stone, tore out of her grip.

"No!" he shouted. He was clawing his way across the wall when she turned, fingers curling into rotten splinters. "I found it! I cannot—"

"What are you doin'?" she cried, snatching at his robe. "Stop it! Whatever it is, it's not worth it. Come on!"

His long, willowy fingers clamped onto her shoulders. "She is afraid of it," he gasped.

"What?" Asha yelped. Fingers like bare bones dug into her arms. She had never seen his eyes so wide or wild.

"The witch. She is afraid of the great beast. Afraid of being near it. If they collide—"

A knotted black limb punched through the wall beside them, ripping the wood away with a heavy swipe. Asha shrieked. Pallas released her like a hawk withdrawing its claws and shoved her away.

"Guard your heart!" he shouted, and raced the other way.

With a screech, the monster surged through the break in the wall. There was no time to watch Pallas disappear. Asha spun and scrambled back down the hall, the small creatures yowling under her feet. She clambered out of the closest window. The frame collapsed beneath her and threw her to the ground. Yelping as her leg throbbed, she somersaulted clumsily and hobbled into another cramped hallway. She didn't stand a chance in the open.

The beast's shriek followed her—and another cry, too. A pained human wail followed her as she crashed into a warped door grown too big for its frame. Both screams stabbed into her, crashing footfalls shaking the ground. She found another window and leapt through; gasps and sobs chased her out of the house. She had a clear path to the trees.

Dim gold eyes appeared in her path.

Something slammed into her chest. She made a noise strange even to her own ears—a gasp, a gurgle.

The beast stood still and calm before her. She looked down at its claws, buried to the wrist in her flesh.

A sob dripped from her mouth. She gripped the gaunt arm, whimpering as she tried to tug it free. Its claws curled into her heart.

Her fingers grew slack and the world disappeared.

She brushes her fingers across his face as he sleeps, his stubble lightly scratching her skin. He's a shadow in the dark, touched by faint moonlight seeping through a crack in the curtains. He stirs under her hand, draping an arm over her shoulder, heavy and comforting.

She edges closer to tuck her head under his chin, but stops when the baby warbles irritably between them. The cold prods at her back as she looks down at that small face, lit under a hint of pale light.

She feels... nothing.

The baby shakes her small fist, stretching and testing this new freedom from her swaddling cloth. Aingael runs a finger over that tiny, silky arm, little feet pummeling her stomach.

Hearne sighs against her ear, half awake, chin cradled against her shoulder. "She'll be runnin' 'fore she's a year," he says groggily, wrapping them in the smell of fresh earth and sweat as he holds them both tighter.

Aingael tilts her head and clumsily kisses his whiskered cheek. Maybe this isn't so—

She spoons three scoops of powder onto the paper with pointed taps, her lips pressed to a thin line. How many times can she forget the measures for a simple fortitude spell, and with the buyer on the way? Her eyes skip over her notes, alternately sharp then idly glazed, and she sighs as she reaches for her mortar.

That piercing screech shoots up her back, again. Her shoulders tighten and she knocks a bottle of fennel seed across the worktable. Sucking in a hard breath, she slaps the bottle, knuckles stinging as it clatters across the floor. The baby shrieks louder.

Aingael grips her ears hard enough to tear them off, leaning her forehead against the bench, and works to breathe—

Her mother coos mindlessly at the baby, bouncing the little one on her hip as Aingael stares sightlessly at the ceiling. She has stopped trying to remember basic spells. Her shop is closed. She thinks she could handle it, if Hearne were to stride over the threshold right now, drop the spoils of his hunt, and wrap her up in his warmth.

But the hunt is not finished. She must be patient, she tells herself, hearing echoes of a dozen relatives casually telling her the same. A hunt can last far longer than expected, if the quarry is illusive.

Yet the village is always full of talk of his hunting prowess. He is the smartest, fastest, most skilled hunter in the clan. Yet prey suddenly eludes him, keeps him away for weeks at a time.

The pit in her stomach, fatter than anything she has ever borne, grows heavier.

She is walking one of the village's outlying paths, thankful for the quiet and the fresh air that fills her chest, when she sees him. And her.

Hearne is lit by soft yellow lamplight, brushing his dipped head and unkempt brown hair. The lamp dangles from a woman's hand—the fourth or fifth daughter of the Bellis clan, fair and willowy. Hearne leans across the back wall of a Bellis cottage, out of view of the main road, enveloping the woman with his sturdy presence. Aingael can't see his face, but the Bellis girl's—warm and smooth and glowing with youth—is filled with a coquettish smile.

Aingael empties her stomach in the bushes outside her home. But the pit in her belly is too great to dislodge.

Aingael sits by the fire, the heat pressing against her back. Her husband left her hours ago with a kiss on the forehead, so absent and inattentive that he may as well not have bothered.

The babe is in her crib, flailing her tiny legs. Pushing the rest of the world out. Trapping her.

Crushing her.

No. That's something else. Aingael's hand shakes as she touches her chest. She can't keep food down. The pit is taking up too much space. It's grown to fill her entire body, a twisting, writhing pain, like a muscle tightened until it rips itself apart.

She does not want to feel it anymore. She does not want to feel anymore.

Her fingers press to her skin—then into it. She flinches, a slight gasp tugging out of her throat. Warmth dribbles down her fingers as they push deeper.

Extract the poison. Heal the wound.

Her eyes blur. She doesn't know if it's from tears or agony. The tips of her fingers brush a hard plate of bone. They push.

The babe is crying. Aingael realizes her silent, open-mouthed gasps are no longer silent. Her hoarse scream fills the house, wall to wall. She grips. And pulls.

Bright. Bright. Light. Blind.

Tingling. Burning. Pain.

Wrong. Mistake. Mistake. MISTAKE.
Shouldn't. Don't.
Too late.

Footsteps. Running. Outside. Away. White, white, white...

He! Love! Home. Finally. Look at me—

Terror. Rage. Scream.

Pain—

The first thing to reach Asha was a sound—a squelch, like flesh being sliced. Hard earth pressed against her temple as the world remade itself out of fuzzy shapes and noises.

Her fluttering eyes caught on the beast as it reeled backward, arm cleaved through and spilling sticky black blood. It collapsed under its own weight, howling.

Hearne, moving with a beastly wrath, stomped down onto its back. The monster writhed and squealed under his weight. Hearne brought his sword down in vicious, blunt swings, like he was chopping firewood. Once, twice, three times.

With a wet thud, the beast's head toppled to the ground.

Hearne's sword followed, tossed away without a thought. He suddenly filled Asha's vision as he fell to his knees at her side.

"Asha," he said, voice shaking. She felt him pulling at her shoulder, turning her over with strained care. He paused. He prodded at the center of her chest like he expected it to cave in. Groaning, she weakly pushed his hand away. That hurt, the idiot.

A sigh shook out of Hearne as he gathered her into his arms. She whined in protest, her mind still a fog, before resting her chin against his shoulder and settling into the embrace. He was warm. It was nice in the cold.

She wasn't sure how long they stayed that way, silent as he stroked the back of her head. Her thoughts were still hazy when he took a deep breath and carefully put her down. He disappeared for a moment and Asha lay still, eyes adjusting to the dark. The abandoned village was there, cold and whispery. Suddenly, something occurred to her, like a half-forgotten memory layering itself over this place. Screams of terror, muted in her mind. Some villagers fleeing as others collapsed and yet others stood unnaturally straight and still. An elegant form floating near the collapsed well, fingers clutching at air.

Hearne's heavy footfalls dispelled those frail wisps of thought. "All right, cub," he murmured. "Come on."

He guided her arms over his shoulders, and she scoffed even through the haze. She hadn't ridden on anyone's back since she was a baby. But she went along with it for his sake, resting heavily against him as he stood and broke into a steady walk.

She was starting to drift off with the rhythm of his steps when he spoke. "I'm sorry," he muttered, more like he was talking to himself than to her. "I'm sorry ya got caught up in this."

His steps made a strange sound, like he was walking with more than two legs. Blinking, she looked down at his side—beneath her, tapping against his knee, hung a sack soaked in black ooze.

Her world darkened. She was too weak to stay awake. Inside her eyelids, she glimpsed a curl of gnarled dark, and wisps of white hair.

"But it'll be all right now. Better than all right," Hearne said as sleep took her. "And then I promise I'll tell ya everything."

A crash and a roar startled Asha awake.

"Sorceress!" Hearne bellowed like he was calling a hunting party to bear. "I've done your bidding."

Asha only got a glimpse of the tower's great door (and the muddy boot print on the pale wood) before they were suddenly in the witch's great hall. It looked different now—the tables laden with oddities were gone, and in their place was a dark-wood throne. The witch perched delicately on its deep red cushions, looking as unmoved and elegant as ever.

"Offer your proof, then," she said, eying Hearne steadily.

Asha swore he growled, near silent but deep enough to feel through his shoulders. "Ya had no business bringing my sister into this." He knelt and shifted Asha off his back, carefully lowering her to the floor. "Add a healin' spell to my payment."

"And yet her safety seems to have motivated you," the witch said flatly. "Perhaps you should be thankful for the encouragement."

Hearne had a way of pressing a fearful amount of anger into stone-faced quiet. Asha could feel him aiming a silent, furious glare at the witch.

"Fine," the witch conceded. "I am feeling generous. Now, your proof?"

In sharp, steady silence, Hearne untied the sack from his belt and tossed it to the floor. Asha watched the burlap fall open. The beast's seeping head looked back, its once golden eyes dull and sightless.

The witch rose from her throne and craned to see, but didn't step closer. Shakily, Asha propped herself up on an elbow. She caught the jerk of Hearne's head, and he was turning to kneel beside her when the witch spoke again.

"Well done," she said, her voice as clear and empty as glass. "I see it was wise to trust you."

Hearne grunted irritably. Asha sat up, hissing as throbs of memory pounded back into her head. The village, the monster, the woman she'd been in a dream...

"I've kept my part of the bargain," Hearne said shortly, folding his arms across his chest. "Now you keep yours."

No answer came. When Asha looked up, one eye shut against the hall's harsh white, the witch was still fixated on the beast's head. Hands delicately folded over her chest, her eyes drifted closed, head tilted back serenely. She might have looked relieved, or happy, if she ever looked like anything.

"My wife!" Hearne roared, the words bursting into a hundred echoes against the tower walls. It made Asha cringe. "Where is she?"

That got the witch's attention. With a graceful tilt of her chin she leveled her gaze at him. Asha couldn't keep her eyes on the witch because Hearne's voice was still bouncing around inside her head, battering through every other thought. The village, the beast, its claws—she gripped her chest, found no hole—the *memories*—

"My," the witch said, "you are a dull one."

Sound abandoned the room, prickling silence filling the space in its wake like the beginnings of a storm. It was a long moment before Hearne spoke. "What?"

"You do not truly believe she could have survived this long, do you?" the witch said smoothly, brushing a hand over the curve of one of her horns. "Ten years, alone, in that forest? Hope has made you a fool. Yet, how strange. You did not care so deeply when she was alive."

Asha stared at the witch's face—her impassive eyes and sharp cheeks. Something tumbled into place in Asha's mind, like a cave collapsing.

"Hearne," she choked, "she's—"

Hearne's blade glided from its sheath with a shrill, metallic *shink*. Asha caught the edge of bared teeth and wild eyes as he stormed to the throne.

"Wait!" Asha screamed. But he was too fast, a single hulking blur rushing forward to slice the witch in two—

He lurched like he'd been punched in the gut, the blade flying from his hand and clattering across the tile. His leg buckled and he collapsed to a knee, gasping like a drowning man.

"You will have no further need of this," the witch said evenly, her hand held high, thin fingers clutching something invisible. Her grip tightened and he cried out, shuddering and choking. "It served to quell that beast, but pain and folly is all it has to offer now."

"Stop!" Asha screeched as she scrambled to his side. "Aingael, stop!"

The witch's head snapped toward her. Hearne, suddenly able to breathe, coughed violently as he fell to his hands and knees.

"It's you," Asha said shakily. "You"—she pointed at the witch, then whirled toward the row of blank-faced guards against the wall—"and they—they were people from that village. Like Pallas. You took out their hearts."

The witch's eyes narrowed.

"That's what the monsters are, aren't they?" Asha asked thickly. Without looking, she pointed to the head still oozing on the tile. "And it—*it* was—"

The words clung to the back of her throat, and her gaze tumbled down to Hearne as he lifted his head. His eyes locked on her, dim with the truth.

He seized violently, too rigid to scream. Asha shrieked as he crumpled to the floor. "*No*—!"

Breath left her in a painful gust. Every part of her tensed to its breaking point. Something wedged in her chest like a dull ax.

"Stupid child," the witch's calm voice pierced Asha's mind. Asha made no sound as she tried to pull air back in, hands flying to her throat. It felt like she was splitting apart.

Guard your heart dripped into her ear.

"Aingael was a fool." The witch's voice rose as Asha collapsed against Hearne's back. Magic hacked at the bone in her chest. "Weak and pathetic. The thrashings of her own wretched heart nearly destroyed her. But I am free. I"—her voice grew and grew to a bellow, an inescapable wave—"am more than she ever could have been!"

The pain ceased. Asha toppled, her chin cracking against Hearne's shoulder, heaving air back into her lungs.

Her head snapped up, and she found streaks of tears staining the witch's face. The witch, dabbing at her cheeks, seemed even more surprised than Asha was. Her eyes locked on the monster's head, confusion scrawled across her face, and Asha realized—you can't cry without a heart.

A crash rocked the tower door. Asha whipped around in time to see the wood clattering in its frame before it was jolted by another staggering blow, then another, and another, harder and louder each time. One final shock and it splintered, bursting in with a rush of cold wind.

One spindly limb dragged a great black body through the gap. The stump of another guided it along like a snapped oar. It had fewer golden globs on its body, some burst and grey, but enough to see by. It moved without any sign of a head.

The beast. Aingael's heart.

Strips of white poked through the flesh of its back. With a slurping sound they pushed out, growing larger and protruding farther. The creature let out an agonized squeal, but the noise came from somewhere else—a chill balled in Asha's stomach when she realized it was the head, suddenly alive and wailing behind her.

With a final yank, feathery wings erupted from the beast's back, dripping with ooze and stretching to twice the size of its body. It lifted itself off the ground with one powerful flap, Asha's hair whipping wildly in its wind.

The witch roared like a possessed thing, her smooth voice jagged and raw with rage. A black-and-white flame bloomed in each of her hands. The beast roared and dove at her, claws outstretched. Between them, Asha could only duck.

A dozen things happened in an instant. Hearne jumped over her, shielding her with his body. Magical fire struck the beast as it sailed overhead. The smell of burnt feathers stung Asha's nose as the beast crashed to the floor, howling, just missing them.

"Kill it!" the witch screamed. The beast rose and slammed its claws against the ground, yowling in answer. The floor kept quaking, and Asha saw a wave of white rushing toward them as the witch's guards charged.

Then there was an arm around her middle and she was hauled from the floor. She squawked as Hearne threw her over his shoulder and sprinted across the tile, out of the heart of the fight and straight for the destroyed door.

"Wait!" Asha cried, slapping his back. He stumbled, but not from the hit.

"We have to go," he managed, the words bleeding out of a pained grunt. She felt him stumble to a knee and her toes touched the ground. She stood straight as he heaved for breath at her feet. His skin was pale as ice. Whatever the witch did, it hurt him too much. "*You* have to go."

Behind him, waves of guards swirled around the beast like rapids around a jutting black rock. The beast flung aside dozens of them with a swing of its remaining arm. Magical fire flashed against its body—it howled, reared and crushed more of the guards underfoot.

Hearne twisted a hand in her coat. "Go."

Asha stared down at him. Her eyes darted to the witch, hands a cyclone of fire. The beast's wings, smoldering and burning inch by inch. Hearne, who stood so tall in her mind, suddenly so small.

She put a hand on his shoulder, squeezed gently, then stepped around him and raced toward the struggle.

He shouted after her, but his voice vanished as she dove into the cluster of bodies. They shifted and whirled, waves of black silk carrying her on their current. A guard sailed through the air and barely missed her. Stumbling back, she dove the other way, flinging herself through the crush.

"You," Asha heard the witch snarling. "You almost killed her. You almost killed both of us!"

A boot smashed into Asha's hip, knocking her to her knees. Another cracked her against the temple. The world swam.

A body dropped beside her, an arrow in its chest. She only gave it a second's thought before crawling through the forest of shuffling legs ahead.

"You wanted to die!" yowled the witch. "You wanted to take me with you." The beast shrieked, some sort of answer Asha couldn't understand.

Hearne's sword glinted a few feet in front of her, dancing against the tile to the beat of a hundred footsteps. She scrambled for it, arm outstretched—then felt a smear of black slime beneath her fingers, spread by skidding feet. The beast's oozing black head sat only an arm's length away.

She is afraid of being near it.

With a shiver from hair to heel, Asha drove her fingers into the head's viscous flesh. It formed perfectly to her hand, making it easy to grip. Springing up, she snatched Hearne's sword and carved a path with wild swipes, the head a living shield.

She was nearly at the throne's steps when the witch finally saw her. A flash of terror rushed across her once elegant face, now full of wild eyes and tangled hair. She screeched with rage, sweeping her arm and knocking Asha back with a violent gust of wind.

Asha bounced off a wall of guards and careened forward again, thrusting the head out like a torch swung at a rabid wolf. The witch stumbled, grace gone, magic spitting from her palms. Asha barely blocked a blast of fire with her fleshy buffer, instantly sick as it squealed in pain.

An arrow sailed past, shattering on the witch's horn. *Hearne*—

Asha saw the thought rush across the witch's face before rage overtook it. With a brutal roar she aimed a gale of fire directly at Asha.

It was too much. Asha's arm snapped to the side, the head tearing from her grasp. A dozen hands snatched at her, pried the sword from her grip and wrapped around her throat. The witch's eyes burned as she raised a hand, clawed fingers ready to sink into Asha's heart.

A rush of wind blew past. The witch's eyes went wide. At the edge of her vision, Asha saw a black mass sailing toward them.

A black and white flame formed in the witch's palm. The guards' grasp went slack. Asha didn't stop to think. She leaped forward and grabbed the witch's hand.

Pain cracked through her like lightning. She didn't hear her own scream as she collapsed, hand splitting and burning with fiery magic. Above her, a gnarled black arm wrapped around the witch's shoulders and drew her into a flurry of feathers and shadow.

And then someone else was there. Suddenly, as if Asha had missed her until now, a woman with long black hair and sharp cheeks faded into being where the two had once been. Her simple, filthy dress fluttered as she tumbled to the floor.

Silence made a husk of the room. Asha heard only the blood pounding in her ears and her own whimpers as she clung to her blistered hand. She cautiously shifted closer.

Aingael stared at the ceiling with unmoving eyes, panting and spasming.

Asha didn't turn away when Hearne's voice boomed behind her, the sound of bodies crashing to the floor trailing after. She didn't move when he grabbed her shoulder, or when he went still beside her. She only looked up when he shifted to Aingael's side, slowly, like he was moving in a dream. He brushed his fingers across his wife's cheek.

Her hands spasmed, quaking as they latched onto his fingers and Asha's charred skin. Asha yelped, tears stinging her eyes, only to feel the cool of a salve spreading across her wound. A golden glow grew between Aingael's hand and hers, then softly ebbed to nothing.

The sprawling hall echoed with a great quiet, as if it had never known a witch at all.

Asha dragged her feet across the dull grey grass, curling and uncurling her freshly healed hand. Hearne stared ahead, dust puffing up under his heavy steps. Even Aingael's twitching against his shoulders wasn't enough to jar him.

He seemed different now. Tired and hunched in a bone-deep way. Or maybe, she thought, echoes of memories that weren't her own drifting through her mind—maybe *she* was different.

It would take her a while to get used to it.

The forest yawned before them, though it didn't seem as frightening as it did before. From here it was only a dozen miles back to the village. Even at this pace they would make it home before dusk.

She looked back at the spiral tower—it was far behind them now, vast and empty, wrapped in an eternal chill. She could just make out black specks spreading out from the doors, the guards shuffling out like ants fleeing a dead hill. She wondered if they'd go looking for their hearts like Pallas did.

Out of the corner of her eye she saw Aingael shudder violently, clinging to Hearne's shoulders. The worst of her spasms had stopped, but every time she started to calm a new wave rattled her again. Asha wondered if the monster and the witch were still fighting inside her—two half-minds that had been without each other for too long.

As they reached the forest's edge, something shifted in the brush, and Asha's eyes snapped to it. A dozen yards away, a man with short black hair stood watching them, arms folded in silky black robes. He nodded when she spotted him.

By the time she recognized him—he looked so different without white hair—Pallas had already moved back with a graceful step, blending into the dark.

"Asha," Hearne said when he noticed her falter. Aingael settled against his back, briefly calm. Staring into the dark a moment longer, Asha shook herself and ran to catch up, walking beside them into the trees.

About the Author

Ashley Reed is a fantasy and science fiction writer who left the forested bogs of her ancestors to bake in the southern California sun. A video game narrative designer by day (and by night), she's also known for short fiction about headless motorcyclists and mummies who fall in love with vampires.

Her favorite places are dark sushi bars, abandoned roller rinks, and foggy forests - anywhere something unusual promises to happen. If you're looking for her, those are some promising places to start.